SWEET SAD SANDAL BOY

SPENCER MIRABAL

For information about permissions to reproduce selections from this book, write to Lit City Press: hello@litcitypress.com.

Books may be purchased in quantity and/or special sales by contacting the publisher, Lit City Press: hello@litcitypress.com.

Published by Lit City Press, Austin, Texas.

Cover Illustration, Design, & Additional Edits © 2019 :
    Martha Boucher. Austin, Texas
    Jordan Raffety. Austin, Texas.
    Morgan Cole. Austin, Texas.

Mirabal, Spencer –

Sweet Sad Sandal Boy : Nonfiction / Poetry / General

ISBN-13: 978-0-578-45261-6 (LIT CITY PRESS)

ISBN-10: 0-578-45261-8

Library of Congress Cataloging Number:

Lit City Press
Printed in the United States of America.

DEDICATION

To my dear friend Sugarbear. For the wine and the yoga mat on your attic floor. For re-reminding me of the path home.

CONTENTS

Drink Pairing Menu

Acknowledgements

About the Author

DRINK PAIRING MENU

Please pair your reading experience with one (or all) of the drinks listed below. Feel free to take breaks & use this chapbook as a coaster. Spilling frequently is both welcomed & encouraged.

BOTTLE OF RED WINE (MALBEC or RIOJA)

Bottle must be no less than $9, but no more than $20. Share with a friend or lover.

QUASI-OVERPRICED BOURBON WITH WARM COKE

2 drink minimum. 5-minute time limit to finish all drinks. Drink alone.
(Warm coke optional)

HOME BREWED COFFEE OR TEA

I

Valentine's Day, 2034

There is music in the living room, which is
nothing new; it's never not
in our house.

Tonight, you put on an exhausted 7-inch
of Donny Hathaway
A Song For You
purrs and pops
warms the room
a bag of kettle corn in a sauna

maybe they're too old for this now, but the
kids making handmade Valentine cards
out of old parchment paper we've collected
a pink plastic bin of
                        bark
                                leaves
                                        seashells
                                                leather
                                stones
                                clay
hand-me-down knick-knacks
hides under the old bunk bed
for evenings like this one
all of it sprawled on the Egyptian rug
my mom bought in 1995
the best *new-parent* money could buy
her gift to us
the night before the wedding
in small company.

Even now, when they could visit a water park
on Neptune, digitally sculpted
programmed in their brain chips
at any time, you insist our children be crafty
Kept engrossed in making everything by hand.

Taught them texture of glitter
how holding it all together in the cupped mug
of your hands could teach you
to love a beautiful mess of another person
while I was off being a fireworks show
you were gifting them mugs
filled with hot lemon balm tea &
lavender; when they came back.

Never-ever-forever-never-do-I
thank you enough for this.

Rest your head on my shoulder
let's slow dance
you love like a lioness.
glitter in your mane
glue caked on your paw
claws on my back
when we sway
never sharp
I'm crooning an
off-tune falsetto
into your eardrum
soft enough to be
a balmy breeze.

I love you in a place where there is no space or time

On our Egyptian rug –
Frosted-Flakes-milk
Argentinian wine stains
all over our space from different times

You've always been so
beautiful at 8:31 PM.

Dandelion Lady

Let's plant dandelions in the yard
precious weeds; let's drink champagne
eat pizza in the park
the sunset a secondary side salad
we brought just in case
let's talk about all of the countries
we hope to travel to
then let's just go to them

I hear Croatia is a cheap trip
a kind of overlooked Italy.

Stop everything at the slightest whiff of a drizzle
let's head to the lake in kayaks
I'm certain of a spring shower
our shared affinity for torrential rains is a baptism
is a heart juicer
only the best nutrients
of ourselves in each other's cups
cups we made and painted
favorite combinations of colors
in our own individual pottery classes

kiss me stupid hard

grab my face with both my palms
tip over your boat
tumble into the lake
kiss me sloppy stupid
till the day meets its end
let your eyes speak lifetimes
naked in your bed
till the night shuts them

eucalyptus candle smoke
through the bedroom at dawn

blends with an old Louisiana cigar
sleeping in the roots of my lamp
made of wicker and oak

you'll floated away
to ride your bike in Texas petrichor
a kind of barbecue, tasting different
in its inhale
of different towns
but on the pillow
your Sunday perfume on the pillow
whispers that your love language
is receiving gifts of scents

Mine is words of future affirmation

I learned it takes fifteen weeks
for dandelions to bloom / I am certain
it'll only take ours five days
it's the same as the act of
our lives mixed together
a phenomenon.

When We Read Together

Only the skin of our elbows touch
I wait for the perfect moment
when we both turn a page
in synchronization.

We have dipped our Velcro bodies
into cold water / picked a nook in nature
to get lost separately
from each our lives

no limbs wrapped
among each other
like the middle of a new, warm
cinnamon pretzel

no lips pulling at the cliff
of your clothes, begging
to have the puzzle pieces of
your shape put together

just our elbows touch
occasionally our breath
in synchronization

Very Serious Questions on Our Second Date

Catawampus is a word
people still use it, right?

Is folding your pizza slices a priority to you?
Follow up question:

      Do you consider deep dish to be pizza?
      Because that might be a deal breaker.

Do you push the toothpaste up
from the bottom of the bottle

with precision and care? Or do you squeeze out
as much as you can / as quick as you can

      from the neck / no thought of preserving it
      worrying over its winded wrinkles

What do you mean am I really talking about toothpaste?
Is our love a see-saw?

Can you pass me my
Quarter-Life Hearing Aids™?

      I've got this bad case of toddler listening skills
      I'm trying to kick this week / month / year.

I hate my lips
shaped like a flattened cathedral bell

Honestly, I hate everything about my face
this dried olive with deployed car airbag cheeks

      covered in the least affluent moss beard.

What do you hate most about yourself?
How quickly can we get back to talking about me?

Do you want to share social security numbers?
I'll pass mine over on a napkin.

> You do the same. You're staying the night
> forever, right? Forever, right?

I spend more time retrying the same three shirts
every morning than actually eating

Is that vanity or anxiety?

Do you like your eggs poached?
Would you like your life poached?

> How would you get me to stop biting my nails?
> Eating toothpicks?
> *Accidentally* starving myself?
> Get the caked self-deprecation
> out of the roof of my mouth?
> Do you like to dye your hair?
> Do you think about dying
> as much as I do? Can I Venmo you
> next week for this?
> Not the therapy.
> The dinner.

II

A Baking Book

When they ask how we met
we'll tell them our romance was a water birth
in the Colorado River; our bodies swam
in cheap sheets in a room where we wished
the walls were white
the floor, a dark, old wood
your olive skin fresh, familiar
my chipped barn door nails
seem less mauled
when I trace them
as if they were rented ice skates
on your back's weakest spots
in the same way we trace the map
to the rest of our lives together
on a canvas, blindfolded.

Maybe our love's better written
our favorite page in a baking book
the homemade croutons one
the rosemary sourdough bread
slow simmered in canola oil one
the handwritten edits and crossed-out compromises one
then throw us on skillet, baby
make something wonderful out of us

Technicolored & Telephoto

the world is carved in a new high-definition
intimate perspective
tortoise tinted glasses; bought, cut and shaped
for my eyes / to breathe easy
having been tired from the strain
searching for the future
in each individual thread
of unwashed pillowcases

driving home – I look up to see
beyond the freeway overpass
a pilgrimage of clouds spun
creamsicle-tangerine-cauliflower

no time to stop and take a picture for you
but *promise's* and I *swears* that the evening kneaded its colors
like pumpernickel dough / the evening molded the clouds
into a peach-tinted mountain / the evening became plum
hued cotton candy / the evening was like the last master
wide sunset scene
of every Disney princess movie's conclusion
wearing dusk like a mother's old wedding dress.

When we get married
Can we have the ceremony in the middle of the freeway?
Can we not tell the town and have cars careen past us
anyone and everyone careening
made sure to know we are absolutely
serious about the *till death do us part* bit?

i love you too...

It was a whisper
when she would say so
a starved whisper
she told me, saying
it scared her
not because
she didn't mean it
but because
when I spoke the words first
I sounded like a bear trap
like an owl cage
so severe
so sure of it.

She Has Returned –
The Chairwoman For The Monthly Meeting
of The Unofficial Committee of Ghosting
On Account Of Holiday Season Guilt
And Unfulfilled Community Service Hours

Unadulterated
Jealousy & Forgiveness
have never
been
can never
be
in the same room
together
with me

my two
longest standing
companions

Who do I allow back
into the house tonight?

Still Cruisin'

We left Montana Bar
    to trek up and down
        the steepest Seattle streets
in tattered Nordstrom Rack boots
    lips manhandled like bald tires
        2 AM winter air giving our bones a glimpse
          of what it must feel like to be
      salmon left a little too long in the freezer
not even your favorite
blueberry dark chocolate Chapstick
        I'm keeping in my jacket pocket
    can seem to keep you close to me
    you're always three steps ahead
    deliriously weaving around
    cracked sidewalks near a
        24-hour QFC grocery store
          and a conversation about
        sexy Winnie the Pooh
      with your friends from years before me
        it all sounds like French.

        or maybe it's more like
          French Sign Language you're using
the last of your voice
      strep throat's been drunk jackhammering
      for these buddies
    your love for their company
      keeping you from sticking dynamite
down your throat to end the party forever
    I can relate to the strep throat
      why would anyone leave you?
    me, with my mouth shut like
      a child-proof jewelry box. Wearing
a frown my mother passed down to me
      Frida brow / Cyclops eye
Will our lives ever meet in the middle?

When is the part where
our separate dearest friends
        meld together with one another
like a perfect shade
    of omelet yellow
        on a palette?
Maybe we're not meant to be
    a museum painting
immortalized by a few
    head-nodded-at by most
        maybe our physical distance
            has created too much
of a lyrical dissonance.
            In one of our 4-hour phone calls
                you called me
            the tentative love of your life
                and man
            that was   really sweet to hear
        when you said it
            but man
        it's a huge   bummer
hearing it in voicemail forever saved
    in my head now.
Maybe our lives are too tectonic.
        Wait, that's not right
            I just looked it up
            it's tectonic shift:
        a slow moving
            of our summer blanket-thin
foundation
            geologists say
knowing when the Earth's plates collide
    helps us understand why and where
events like earthquakes occur
        and volcanoes erupt
Would you rather I was an earthquake
or a volcano?
    Which one of those is more exciting for you?
        Which one
        lasts longer?

SWEET SAD SANDAL BOY

             How much longer
          are we going to fucking walk
until

we are home.
Finally in bed.
You nuzzle your
snow tire cheek
into my boney, cold concrete
left shoulder and breathe out
You are always so warm
before you kiss me.
Felt the muscles of
your lips form a smile
in-between sleepy kisses
like the way children are
overcome with glee sometimes
when they can't help themselves.
Pass me the strep throat.
We're still cruisin'

A Summer Downpour

I am an escape for you
a VR, POV porn
of doggy-style to you
indulge in me for a while
then delete your browser history
before anyone knows
where you were
While you are in my life
I am an anxious chameleon
not quite sure of what to be afraid of
specifically, so I become
the color of thunder
I feel every earthquake measured
by the Richter scale
in all of recorded history
all at once
I am the doubt of the benefit
I wear a black cape and dangle over
industrial ledge above a vat of green acid
daring you to throw me in
make me a manic super villain
while you are in my life
I am rusted platinum
I am three months of dry heaving
I am Brian Wilson's bed sores
I am a deep breath of Saturn's atmosphere
I am cataract surgery without anesthesia
I am a tumor removal
done by a barber with Parkinson's
I am a crucified cockroach begging
for it all to be happening for a purpose
I am myself in a dream where I drive
off of a towering interstate overpass, careen
into the ground; don't wake up
dying in real life, not in the dream

But when you leave my life
I will become you to someone else.
I will be a leech that has latched onto itself
in a perfect circle, starving.
You wanted the rain?
This is the rain.

III

St. Petersburg, Florida

new heartbreak at a wedding is a
mosaic cardboard coffee coaster
a sweet arrangement all soaked
indigo eye bags
cold-brewed sadness
my hair all buzzed off
uncle John eats cake
glee fills his cheeks
for the first time in months
grandma Anne dances
recently celebrating her 53rd 29th birthday
when she smiles at me / her eyes peel away
my chameleon skin
my moldy potato skin
her smile wrinkles weave
a basket to hold
my dying body
my colorless body
cousin Peter, king of the evening spring wedding
in St. Petersburg, Florida
watches his adoptive father, Jeff
give the sweetest, most remarkable speech
neither of them know that the words are repurposing
the rubble of me / once a marble statue
into a shower in a homeless shelter
into a post-funeral puppy / into a selfless gift

your damp blonde hair on my chest
a morning in Bozeman on your bed tucked
in the corner near the window

all of Jeff's words crumble into expired porridge
pours from my head out my ears down my body
is my body even here right now?
is today the wedding?
is it Saturday?

how many days have i been here?

later / or earlier (who's to say)
i walk on an April beach the color of white
only saved for master bedroom linens
the banyan trees sun kissed
made both shades of chartreuse
made komorebi
the sky a bath bomb of blue
Egyptian / Royal / Cornflower / Powder
the clearest tide on my ankles is
a familiar left hand running through my hair
from the back of my head to front
only to comb back to the collective of the ocean
it feels like night when i confessed to loving
the sensation of your fingers rubbing my earlobe
only for you to leave me three weeks later
Linda asks mom if she can open a tiki bar
        when they move to Key West together
my mom laughs and smiles at her wife
my mom will die in Key West someday, probably
i ask her if Linda is the love of her life & her best friend
because that's how i thought it was supposed to be
she's not sure of what guidance to give me
what treasure map in rushed cursive
to pass on to me

how many days have i been here?

earlier / or later (who's to say)
i am in a white, porcelain hotel shower
i stand in the corner where the water can't touch me
the mood set by music that cyclones into
liquid version of you that
sticks its whole hand in my ear
chokes an ear infection into existence
smack myself in the face with my palms like ping pong
        paddles so that maybe i'll have a seizure
shock these images of you

out of my corroded VHS tape brain

a shower in north Austin
we stand in the corner
teaching one another how to wash a lover's back
kiss under warm, wet pellets

i'll never kiss anyone in a shower again
depression isn't sadness
sadness isn't an aesthetic
it's just exhausting
i hate seeing you everywhere you're not
my eyes hurt / i want to scoop my eyes out
like stubborn ice cream
scraping them out
it's so hot here

how many days have i been here?

Oops, I'm Sad Now

Mouth full of owls
I was a quail on fire
with a mouth full of owls
apologized in braille
that is to say
I was a photocopy
of a fax
of the braille dictionary
non-existent
that is to say
my words tumbled out
like a decaying hospice patient
down a bone dry
water slide
messy
painful to watch
empty of effort
but all of it was
really to say that
parasitic are
promises
and kisses
from empty
people

fuck me
but not actually
please leave
but not actually

I am really going to ruin
your god damn life briefly
come back in twenty years
I'll finally be a tangerine tree

Hymn for Judas

Dear friend
Quick
Hurry

I need a circumstance to exist in

I'll lease my body to a summer
southern mythos of myself

Look at me build a makeshift throne
of Dominos Hawaiian pizza boxes

Watch me portray a conjoined twin octopus
flailing all 16 of my arms for women
for vices I've never needed

unfiltered cigarettes

Nine Coronas in a night

Stomach ulcer? Never heard of her

Gin & tonics in bed

Back out on doing shrooms
puke bacon-wrapped jalapeños
tequila on Labor Day

Ouchie

Whatever is left of the me you miss
becomes a cranberry wine stain
on your beige raincoat
you'll never want to wash away

Sweet friend

don't go

Is your 2 week free trial of me up?

All these bizzaro vignettes
must be the scraps of
failed ditched itinerary
but they're mine now

Please screenshot these wild nine-second miseries of me
print them / papier-mâché them / onto a balloon
in the shape of my face all cartoon-like

Watch me fashion a noose
out of Texas humidity
possessive jealousy
self-medicated malnourishment

Watch me

Alone in desert

Drunk driving on a treadmill

Belting a hymn for Judas

Can you hear it?

Can you hear it?

The miles between us are more than a distance now

Don't waste your time at the funeral

just Fed-Ex some tulips

Death Has No Time For Vanity

Death does not wait for us to be ready.
Death has no time for vanity.

2 AM in the drive-thru, I learn that you've died
scroll through a digital obituary in my palm
it is not profound to speak of how social media
is separating us, how else would I have known?
How else would you have apologized?
How else could I have I become the quietest tornado
not knowing your house held suicide down in the cellar?
How else would I become a deaf ghost
did the opposite of haunting you long enough
for you to become a real one?
How else could you have become a snowbank
waiting for children's hugs to cave you in?

How did you do it? How did you kill yourself?
That's the part no one is going to talk about
I need to know; how did you kill yourself?
Were you growing your hair out to weave a noose?
Because that's what I've been doing.
That could've been me. That
could be me. But Death
has no time for vanity.
Death does not wait
for us to be ready.

She blares her horn from the car behind me
its back seat stacked to the ceiling
with a war-chest of convenience food wrappers.
She is an old woman; smokes two cigarettes
She shortchanges my cheap grief
shouts to make sure I know
what I am feeling is
insignificant

WE'RE ALL TIRED
WE'RE ALL HUNGRY
    THIS SHOULDN'T BE
        THAT HARD

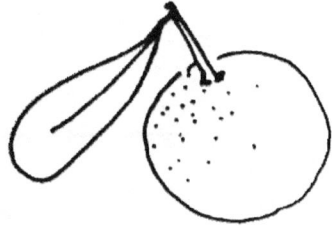

IV

West America

Everyone here will tell you
about the city of books on Burnside street
how November knits leaves yellow and red
like a handmade blanket
for Mother Nature's living room
how the coast is best cold
with a sky like a grey watercolor painting.

But everyone here also has a secret love of their life
A pizza shop where they toss dough in the window
The pastel towers of a bridge crossing the Willamette
River
A hotdog from a basketball game at the Rose Garden
The grass hill behind an old red brick elementary school
A watermelon and tiger's blood Sno cone
near the pool in Grant Park
The smell of the first October overcast
Those blueberry and raspberry bushes in the front yards
of those two houses on Northeast 32nd Court.

Everyone here knows that
there is a time to be here
and a time not to be.

Nothing and nobody we love
is here anymore.

But everyone here also knows that
when they come back they are
evergreen again.

That when a storm rages
they only need to dig their roots deeper.

Amtrak Cascades Alone
For Presumably The Last Time

She gets on in Edmonds
        He gets on in Seattle
the train headed southbound
in a reflection only viewable from the window seat
woman, cheeks of some kind of purple
silver sea shell, listens intently
to a man sitting across from her
her earnest eyes hold onto his words
like a glass of *saved for years just for tonight* Rioja
slow dance swirling with them
when he laughs, she breathes it in
a bowl of chicken noodle soup with carrots and celery
      becomes a warmth whirlpool
drains away all of her
embarrassing stories
her mild vices her slugs
made a home of her
dampest insecurities

It's been a while. A baker's dozen of lifetimes.

They talk and they talk and they laugh and they talk
all the while, Olympia sun took an Ambien
with a double well whiskey / passed out
behind the mountains and the mountains
took the opportunity to throw a party
turn into Venus all yellow and brown
like a premature Thanksgiving disco ball
all of the children on the train become warthogs
trampling and barreling into each other
while wearing name tags with sophisticated scribble
they've been learning like some kind of
ruckus-themed block party and harbor seals
who haven't been home in a while
got drinks with barnacles still chilling

on the dam of rocks along the tracks
neither of them having jobs with health insurance yet
neither of them with anything in common anymore.

But the woman's eyes have no questions for these things.

Only for the man so different than before across her
together in their own cozy moment underneath
        spacetime's comforter.
How long has his hair been pepper speckled
and summer seasoned?
How many
hotel rooms in how many cities has the left side of his
bed been empty?
Have his eyes always been green?
Has this always been the place
they were meant to be

when they find out?

Seattle > Austin // September 2016

this little girl's hand grips her mother's
as if it were a rubber hold on a rock climbing wall
tears down her cheek / quiet creek
        carving a valley of empathy
from the full itinerary
        the leaving, the uncertain
in the gap between the tunnel and the plane
this little girl's mother folds both palms
of cold dough in a pizzeria fridge
        educates her daughter
of the act in kissing their center
                planting them
on the nose of the journey
        thanking it for
everything
    the tumultuous
        the relief
this little girl's eye
        a pond
predictably grey clouds becoming
an elephant stampede
Christmas wish kittens
strawberry crepes on a Saturday
a giant primary-colored parachute in a gym
the grey plastic shut over the pill-shaped window
her ten fingers become crayons
using colors never imagined
        until now
            her mother quiet
in the teaching
    in the flying.

Gratitude To The Jellyfish
For Leaving

Heartbreak is gone
when you find yourself
more fond
of a shirt
she often wore
than her

a deep Atlantic
short sleeved button up
with the white track and
field vertical stripes
the maroon / green floral pattern
looking like someone had
picked them from a jungle
steam pressed
into a cloud
ocean & sky
like a polyester blend.

Breakfast Records

you measure out Forty-Four grams of
your favorite coffee beans
hints of
        jasmine
        caramel
        tangerine
(not quite at the point in your life to
actually taste those flavors)
grind them
way too early in the morning
in a second-hand grinder in a fourth-hand house
pick a mug from a cabinet of mismatched memories
your sink chock full of other's anxieties that are
becoming yours, so you tilt the kettle at a wonky angle
fill it with the sleepy city's water
boil
Two-Hundred-Five degrees
pour
through paper into the glass Chemex
swirl
rinse in the light of a window, an all-too-brief rainbow
the backyard, a jungle
the porch, a junkyard.
the counter, a mess of wet pumpkin-patch bark
from grounds spilled from since-childhood hand tremors
Seven Hundred grams.
Four Minutes.
you're never certain if today is the day
it's all exact, but
doesn't matter

You are at the church of yourself now.

mistake-ridden meditation
quiet chemistry.

Wait for the brew to decide its identity
Blink in slow motion
Feel time's curve

Put your favorite breakfast record on.

Shuffle your feet
in a dance no one will ever see
but your kitchen and
the cul-du-sac cat that
sleeps on the worn beer pong table
abandoned in the yard

when it's ready
pour the coffee into your memory mug
breathe it in to the bottom of your lungs
watch the fog on your glasses inhale / exhale

Drink your worth in.
You are at the church of yourself.
You are allowed to be
at the church of yourself.

ACKNOWLEDGMENTS

Oceans of thanks to Jean Mirabal for championing me through every step of my life, and for telling my writing tutor twenty or so years ago "don't teach him how to write, teach him how to *love* writing." Gratitude, gratitude, GRATITUDE to the countless family, friends and strangers who (sometimes unknowingly) made a direct impact on the words in these poems. You were all life-saving compasses for me in such a strange time in my life. Special thanks to Stephanie Campbell and Joe Brundidge. Both of you were so crucial in ensuring a butterfly effect like no other. Cheers & thanks to Sybil Journal, in which some of the poems in this chapbook first appeared. And to Jordyn Raffety. The sweetest lady. Loving you has always been and continues to be the greatest adventure of my lifetime.

ABOUT THE AUTHOR

Spencer Mirabal is an American filmmaker and poet originally from Portland, Oregon. Now residing in Austin, Texas, Spencer works as the Artistic Director of Chicon Street Poets: a literary arts nonprofit encouraging writers of all mediums to share their work and develop their craft. He balances the rest of his time with eating pizza in bed, drinking pour over coffee from his beloved collection of mugs, meticulously curating seasonal Spotify playlists, and being generally exhausted.